Dear Parent:
Your child's love of reading starts here!

Every child learns to read in a different way and at his or her own speed. Some go back and forth between reading levels and read favorite books again and again. Others read through each level in order. You can help your young reader improve and become more confident by encouraging his or her own interests and abilities. From books your child reads with you to the first books he or she reads alone, there are I Can Read Books for every stage of reading:

SHARED READING
Basic language, word repetition, and whimsical illustrations, ideal for sharing with your emergent reader

BEGINNING READING
Short sentences, familiar words, and simple concepts for children eager to read on their own

READING WITH HELP
Engaging stories, longer sentences, and language play for developing readers

READING ALONE
Complex plots, challenging vocabulary, and high-interest topics for the independent reader

ADVANCED READING
Short paragraphs, chapters, and exciting themes for the perfect bridge to chapter books

I Can Read Books have introduced children to the joy of reading since 1957. Featuring award-winning authors and illustrators and a fabulous cast of beloved characters, I Can Read Books set the standard for beginning readers.

A lifetime of discovery begins with the magical words "I Can Read!"

Visit www.icanread.com for information
on enriching your child's reading experience.

Flat Stanley and the Very Big Cookie. Text copyright © 2015 by the Trust u/w/o Richard C. Brown a/k/a Jeff Brown f/b/o Duncan Brown. Illustrations by Macky Pamintuan, copyright © 2015 by HarperCollins Publishers. All rights reserved. Printed in the United States of America. No part of this book may be used or reproduced in any manner whatsoever without written permission except in the case of brief quotations embodied in critical articles and reviews. For information address HarperCollins Children's Books, a division of HarperCollins Publishers, 195 Broadway, New York, NY 10007.

Library of Congress catalog card number: 2013953796
ISBN 978-0-06-218979-0 (trade bdg.) — ISBN 978-0-06-218978-3 (pbk.)
Typography by Sean Boggs

15   16   17   18   PC/WOR   10 9 8 7 6 5 4 3 2   ❖   First Edition

I Can Read!

READING 2 WITH HELP

FLAT STANLEY

and the Very Big Cookie

created by Jeff Brown

by Lori Haskins Houran

pictures by Macky Pamintuan

HARPER

An Imprint of HarperCollinsPublishers

Stanley Lambchop lived
with his mother,
his father,
and his little brother, Arthur.

Stanley was four feet tall,

about a foot wide,

and half an inch thick.

He had been flat ever since a bulletin

board fell on him.

People in Stanley's town

liked having a flat boy around.

Especially since Stanley

was always willing to lend a hand.

Or even a whole arm.

He helped the librarian reach books

that slipped under the stacks.

He helped the dentist smooth out the new wallpaper in his office.

And when the baker was busy,
Stanley helped him frost cakes—
two at a time.

But one day, Stanley and Arthur
went to Pete's Sweets
and found that the baker
wasn't busy at all.

"What's wrong?" asked Stanley.

"It's the baker in the next town,"
said Pete.

"He's taking away all my business!"

"But how?" Stanley asked.

"What does he have that you don't?"

"Two words," Pete said. "Cake pops."

"Oh, cake pops! Yummy!" said Arthur.

Stanley elbowed his brother.

"What?" Arthur said. "They are!"

"It's true," said Pete glumly.

"They are yummy."

"So why don't you bake

them too?" suggested Stanley.

"I never copy another baker," said Pete.

"I'm the one with the big ideas!

The tart trend?

I started that.

The cupcake craze?

Me again!"

Then Pete held up a flyer.

"This is my chance to get back my customers," said Pete. "I have to think of the next big idea by Saturday." He threw his hands in the air. A cloud of flour flew up. "If I don't, my bakery is doomed!"

That night, Stanley and Arthur tried

to think of an idea for Pete.

Mini muffins? Bite-size brownies?

Everything had been done before.

"How about a nice coconut macaroon?"

suggested Mrs. Lambchop.

The boys didn't know

what a macaroon was.

But it didn't sound like anything

that could beat a cake pop.

The next day was Friday.
Stanley and Arthur stopped
by the bakery after school.

It was a mess!

There was frosting everywhere.

One whole table was covered

with cookie dough.

Candy balls rolled around

on the floor.

"Mr. Pete?" called Stanley.

"What's going on? WHOA!"

Stanley slipped on a candy ball.

His flat arms made a windmill

as he tried not to fall!

Pete came out of the kitchen
just in time to see Stanley land—
SMACK!
Face-first in the cookie dough!

Arthur peeled his brother off the dough.

There was a Stanley-shaped dent in it.

"I'm so sorry, Pete!" said Stanley.

But Pete was staring at the dent

with a strange smile on his face.

"The next big idea!" he said.

"It's . . . *big*!"

Pete started racing around the bakery.
The boys didn't know exactly
what his plan was, but they pitched in.

Stanley and Arthur helped mix
a giant batch of cookie dough.
They rolled it out on the table.

Then Pete pulled up a chair.

"Stanley, would you climb up here

and fall on the dough again?"

"Okay," said Stanley.

"But does it have to be

face-first this time?"

Pete grinned and shook his head.

Stanley got up on the chair.

He took a deep breath

and fell backward.

"Perfect!" said Pete.

"Arthur, pull away the extra dough!"

Pete and Arthur pulled and pulled.

Then they helped Stanley stand up.

On the table lay a gingerbread boy.

It was four feet tall,

about a foot wide,

and half an inch thick.

"Just like you," Arthur told Stanley.

"Only good-looking!"

The cookie looked even better
when it was baked and decorated.
"Wow," said Stanley.
"This might sound weird,
but I want to take a bite of
my head."

"Not now!" said Pete.

"We have three dozen

Kid-Size Cookies to make!"

The next morning was the Food Fair.
The Lambchops walked down
Main Street.
"Look at that!" said Mr. Lambchop.
There was a huge crowd
outside Pete's Sweets.
They were waiting to buy
Kid-Size Cookies!

But there were two cookies

that weren't for sale.

"These are for you," said Pete.

"Thanks for saving the day!"

"I always knew I had
the *sweetest* boys in the world!"
said Mrs. Lambchop.
The boys groaned . . .

and took a bite.